Dear Parents,

As the creator of **Go! Go! Sports Girls** and the founder of **Dream Big Toy Company**, I would like to thank you for giving your child the gifts of reading and healthy life-skills.

Healthy habits start early. I created **Go! Go! Sports Girls** as a fun and educational way to promote self-appreciation and the benefits of daily exercise, smart eating and sleeping habits, self-esteem, and overall healthy life-skills for girls. Author Kara Douglass Thom and illustrator Pamela Seatter have taken this dream a step further by creating a series of fun and educational books to accompany the dolls. Now your child can **Read & Play.**

The books have been written for the child who has begun to read alone, and younger children will enjoy having the stories read to them.

I believe every child should have the opportunity to **Dream Big and Go For It!**

Sincerely,

Jodi Bondi Norgaard

Jodi Bondi Norgaard

For our very own sports girls
Grace, McKenna, Kendall, Jocie Claire,
Kaelie, Maia, and Michaela,
and their brothers Peter, Ben, Blake,
and Alex, who inspire us every day.
— JBN, KDT, PS, SRB

First published in 2014

Series Editor: Susan Rich Brooke

Text © 2014 by Kara Douglass Thom

Illustrations © 2014 by Pamela Seatter

Jodi Norgaard, Founder and C.E.O.
Dream Big Toy Company™
PO Box 2941, Glen Ellyn, IL 60138

www.gogosportsgirls.com

Library of Congress Control Number: 2013951444

First Edition

8 7 6 5 4 3 2 1

This book was printed in 2015 at Luk Ka Packaging Co., Ltd.
in Street No. 98, Lijia Road, Henggang, Longgang Dictrict,
Shenzhen, Guangdong, China.

ISBN 978-1-940731-02-5

One Step at a Time

Written by Kara Douglass Thom
Illustrated by Pamela Seatter

Dream Big Toy Company™

I was dancing on top of an elephant's head. Not just any old elephant—an African elephant, the biggest elephant of all! My elephant walked while I whirled and twirled. We were a hit! I was dazzled by the lights and the cheering crowd. I could hear them chanting my name: "M.C.! M.C.! M.C.!"

Anyone Can Dance!

Dancing is movement that expresses feelings. Since the beginning of time, cultures around the world have used dance to entertain, tell stories, and celebrate.

"M.C.!" Mrs. Harper's voice came through the crowd.

Suddenly, my elephant was gone. So were the bright lights, my glittery costume, and my adoring fans. Now all I could see were the other dancers in my class, snickering.

"Maria Camila, please pay attention while I teach the dance steps," said Mrs. Harper. "You'll need to know the dance by heart before the recital."

Pay attention. I hear that a lot—from Mrs. Harper, from my teachers at school, and from my Mom and Dad. Everyone is always telling me to pay attention.

I try to pay attention. Really I do. But it's just too hard when so many exciting things happen inside my head. I can fly to Mars in my own spaceship. I can create cheerleading stunts to try out with my friend Roxy. My elephant and I can win the grand prize in a talent show!

"Girls, I'm going to go over the steps once again," Mrs. Harper said from the front of the studio. "And this time, I want you to listen with your eyes closed. Imagine each step in your head as I say it. Picture yourself doing it."

I closed my eyes and tried really hard not to see my elephant.

"We'll begin in first position, arms down low, like you're holding a big round balloon," said Mrs. Harper. "Bring your arms up to fifth position, as if your balloon is rising in the air. Keep those arms rounded above your head. Don't let the balloon slip between your hands!

"Next, bring your right foot up to *passé*. Balance! Now straighten your leg as you bring your foot down, in *tendu*. As your toes touch the floor, let go of your balloon and open your arms to second position.

"Then bring your right foot back to first position and your arms down low again with another big imaginary balloon. Now, we'll repeat that on the other side."

Ballet Basics

1st Position **3rd Position** **5th Position**

2nd Position **4th Position**

I listened as hard as I could, and I tried
to picture what Mrs. Harper was saying.
I even made my elephant sit
out for the rest of dance class.

"Okay, girls, open your eyes," Mrs. Harper said. "Did you see yourself dance in your mind? Who would like to demonstrate?"

Please don't pick me, please don't pick me, I thought. I looked away from Mrs. Harper and glanced over at Roxy. She always remembered the steps. Finally, Kate raised her hand. Phew!

We all watched Kate as she moved from one step to the next. Kate is not only a dancer, but also a basketball player. She says that learning dance steps is just like learning basketball plays.

When Kate finished, Mrs. Harper turned on the music. I was in the back row so I could follow the dancers in front of me. I could still see my elephant sitting in the corner, waiting for me to climb back on his head.

At the end of class, Mrs. Harper handed each of us a CD of our recital song. "Be sure to practice at home!" she said. I think she said it extra loud to me.

Dress Like a Dancer

Many dance classes require tights and a leotard. Your teacher might let you add extras like a skirt, short sweater, or leg warmers. You might also need special shoes, like ballet slippers, tap shoes, or jazz shoes.

Don't wear jewelry or any long, loose items that could move around when you jump. Pull short hair back with a headband or barrettes. Put long hair up in a ponytail or bun.

The best place to dance at my house is right by the front door. To make room, I had to scoot a table into the hall and push a bench into the kitchen. That made a loud **screeching** noise. Then there was a loud **crashing** noise when a picture frame fell to the floor.

"Maria Camila, what in the world is going on?" my dad said as he tried to make his way onstage, only to trip over the bench.

"I need to practice, Daddy. I have to learn a whole dance before the recital. There are just too many steps!"

"How many steps do you do at one time?" my dad asked.

"There must be a zillion."

"You do a zillion steps at one time?"

"Well, no. I just do one step at a time."

"Exactly," said Daddy. "Just one step at a time. That's how you'll learn it, and that's how you'll remember it, and that's how you'll perform the dance at the recital. One step at a time."

Taking dance class is so different from dancing on my own, or making up hip-hop moves with my friends. Usually I can remember what my feet need to do, but I forget what my hands need to do. Mrs. Harper calls the way we move our arms *port de bras*, which makes me giggle. It's French for "carriage of the arms." All ballet steps are French words. I speak French to my elephant, too.

I practiced *passé* and *tendu*, and I remembered my *port de bras*, too. My elephant sat and watched, and he trumpeted politely when I was done. Then my baby brother crawled in and clapped his hands. I gave him a curtsy to say thanks, even though he claps for everything.

French Lesson

- *Tendu* ("to stretch") is extending a pointed foot along the floor to the front, side, or back.

- *Passé* ("to pass") is pointing the toes of a bent leg and touching them to the knee of a straight leg.

- *Plié* ("to bend") is bending both knees.

- *Relevé* ("to rise") is raising your heels off the floor after a *plié*.

- *Chassé* ("to chase") is a skipping step to the front, side, or back.

At the next class, Mrs. Harper went over everything we already learned. When we practiced to music, I was in the front row. This time there were no dancers in front of me to follow—but thanks to the mirror, I could see the other dancers behind me.

Then Mrs. Harper added two more steps: *plié* and *relevé*. They weren't too hard for me to remember. And we did each of those steps twice through. We practiced our combination so many times that day I was sure I knew it by heart—until Mrs. Harper asked us to turn around and face the wall instead of the mirror!

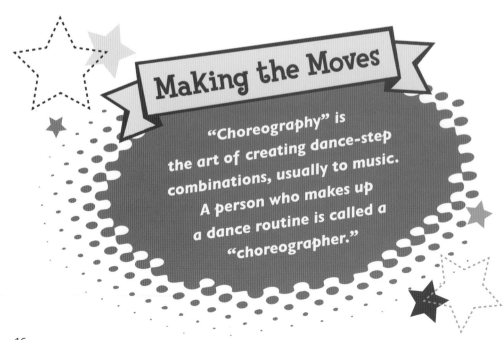

Making the Moves

"Choreography" is the art of creating dance-step combinations, usually to music. A person who makes up a dance routine is called a "choreographer."

Mrs. Harper could see that some of us were terrified of turning around. I really needed the mirror to see what I was doing. Plus, my elephant was sitting in the back of the room, staring right at me. What would I do if he wanted to dance, too?

"Okay, take a minute to close your eyes again," said Mrs. Harper. "I'll turn on the music. Go through the steps in your mind. Make a movie in your head."

I could see myself do the dance in my head. And I refused to let my elephant dance with me. But even so, when we turned to face the wall and started to dance, I messed up. ***A lot.***

"It's hopeless!" I said to Dad on the way home. "I'll never learn the dance. I forbid you and Mom to come to the recital."

"Sweetheart, the recital is still three weeks away. You have plenty of time."

I ♥ Dance

I made a face from the back seat. That was easy for him to say—he didn't have an elephant to deal with.

That night, I practiced at home till my legs and arms ached. I was too tired to dance anymore. I was too tired even to think. I flopped down on my bed, closed my eyes, and just listened to the music.

And after a while, something funny happened. I didn't have to try to imagine the steps. The song itself painted a picture of the dance in my mind.

If I listened closely, the music told me what steps to do next. Every note and every beat was a clue for me.

Dance Spotlight

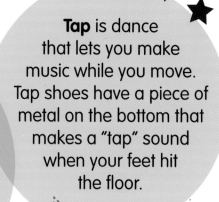

Ballet is a classical dance. It uses an established set of steps, put together in flowing combinations. Many dancers take ballet before learning other types of dances.

Tap is dance that lets you make music while you move. Tap shoes have a piece of metal on the bottom that makes a "tap" sound when your feet hit the floor.

At the next class, we practiced what we learned, without the mirror again. This time I remembered all the steps as the music played— one step at a time. Maybe there weren't a zillion steps after all.

I was imagining myself up on stage in my tutu when Mrs. Harper told us the next part of the dance. "I want you to *chassé* four times in a circle to your right. Then chassé in a circle four times to your left."

What? Oh no! What's a chassé *again? Did she say five times?* I had heard Mrs. Harper talk, but I knew I hadn't really listened.

"Do you want me to tell you again?" Mrs. Harper asked the class.

I looked around the room. A few of the girls were nodding their heads, so I did, too.

Mrs. Harper repeated the instructions as she walked through the steps. This time, I listened. She told us to pretend that we were each moving around the shore of our own round pond of water.

If our circles were too small, we could fall in our ponds. And if our circles were too big, we could fall in someone else's pond. Each circle had to be just right.

"M.C., can you show us?"

My face got hot.

"You can do this," Mrs. Harper said.

I took a deep breath. I reminded myself which side is my right side.

And then, I started to *chassé* in a circle. Four times to the right, round and round and round and round. Then, four times to the left. I was careful not to fall into my pond, or into anyone else's.

"*Brava*, Maria Camila!" Mrs. Harper said as she clapped her hands.

Each time I went to class, I learned a little bit more of the dance. Then at home, I practiced. I practiced during recess at school, too. I practiced so much that the dance became something I knew how to do as well as climbing the monkey bars or writing my name in cursive.

Now that I could remember all the steps, I stopped worrying and started having fun.

I even told my parents they could come to the recital after all.

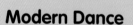

Dance Spotlight

Hip Hop is dance set to hip-hop music. It uses original steps, often with different parts of the body moving in different directions at the same time.

Modern Dance is an expressive dance form. The entire body usually moves smoothly throughout the dance. Sometimes modern dancers do their moves lying on the floor!

Jazz is an upbeat dance inspired by music you might hear on the radio. It uses original steps and changes with the times.

Finally, it was time for the performance! My costume was even more beautiful than I imagined it would be.

We took our places on the stage. I was a little nervous about dancing for a real audience. But I wasn't afraid I would forget the steps. As long as I listened, the music would tell me what to do next.

Right before the curtain rose, Mrs. Harper whispered, "Take it one step at a time. And smile!" Then the music started and the lights went on. It was time to shine.

And I did! I did the whole dance just right, without a mirror—and without my elephant. Of course, he was in the audience, clapping next to my baby brother.

Here's What M.C. Learned:

Being a good listener is a skill, just like dancing is.

Practicing in your mind, or "making a movie in your head," can help you remember the steps.

When something seems too hard to do, break it down into smaller pieces. Focus on one step at a time.

The more you practice, the more confident you'll feel.

Dancer Girl M.C.'s Healthy Tips:

Warm up. Dancers take time to bend and stretch their muscles before they start to dance.

Eat up. Natural snacks like an apple or yogurt give you more energy than sugary snacks.

Drink up. Make sure you replace the water you lose when you sweat in dance class with water, not sodas or sugary drinks.

Cover up. Wear stretchy clothing that allows your body to move, and the right kind of shoes (or bare feet!) for the type of dance.

Rest up. Get lots of sleep every night, especially before a performance.

Dream Big and Go For It!